THOUGHTS THAT SHAPED YOU

Booksquirrel Publications

Book*Squirrel* Publication

Regd. Under MSME Act.

Thoughts that shaped you

By: Piyush Masih and Pallabi Ram

Book Formatting- Rubal Choudhary

ISBN: 978-93-89557-23-7

1st Edition

<u>ACKNOWLEDGEMENT</u>

The completion of this anthology would not have been possible without the incredible rate of work and help of the entire co-authors team whose names cannot be mentioned. To say thanks it would be putting it mildly.

This anthology is based on some handpicked poems and short stories by some writers around the country that will definitely going to touch the hearts of the reader.

A special thanks to Rubal Choudhary, Neha Mondal,Shraddha Upadhyay, Fabbeha Khursheed, Abhishek Patel, Satyadeep Mohanta and Keerthana Dhakshina Moorty for their constant presence throughout the entire project and the entire co-author team as well.

A ton of thanks to the team- Book Squirrel Publishers, without you this would not have been possible.

Above all thanks God Almighty, for your endless, unequivocal love.

<u>DISCLAIMER</u>

This anthology is a work of fiction. The compilers have tried their best to check for plagiarism in the write-ups of all the co-authors contributing to this book.
All the write-ups in this book are unique.
However, if something has escaped my eye and plagiarism is detected at a later date, I shall not be held liable for the same.
We have asked our dear authors to contribute only their original and unpublished works, and our relationship is based on utmost good faith.

COMPILERS

<u>PIYUSH MASIH</u>

Hailing from the city of Sangam of three rivers Ganga, Yamuna and Saraswati- Prayagraj, Piyush Masih is pursuing his career as Engineering Student. Studying in Prayagraj itself. Contributing to two anthologies in which one of the books rewarded the title of World Records. He started writing as a hobby but now pursuing it as an interest and looking forward to be an author. You can check up his write-ups and to know more about this budding writer you can contact him on:

Contact him through Gmail:piyushmasih002@gmail.com
Instagram: @_this.is.piyush_

<u>Soul Mate</u>

You are the sun of my day
The moon of my night,
My pain healer and a sharer of every bite.
The way you handle my pain,
The way you handle me
It's all magical.
The time i cry, the time i shout
You are the one who shut my mouth
The one who always picks my call
Either its 3 at dawn or 4 at noon.
The owner of the magical voice
That makes the soul calm and mind go rest.
The one for whom this heart beats
And breaths are taken...
Would love to spend my now
and then with you till my last breath.

PALLABI RAM

Pallabi Ram daughter of Mr. Jagdish Ram and Mrs Asha Ram was born in West Bengal. She is 19 years old and currently pursuing English Literature Honours. She started writing two years before. She is a co-author of many anthologies. Apart from writing she loves to read novels, cooking, travelling. She keeps strong faith in God.

She is an ambivert person. She always keeps people around her happy. Her life's motive is to be a news anchor.

Contact her through Email - kumaripallavi5539@gmail.com

Instagram - @pallavi8628

<u>Goin' Back Home</u>

Goin' Back Home Comin' Alone
In A Crowd Of Travellers
Holding A Novel; On Earphones
High On Music With A Story
Something The World Calls A Glory
But I'm Sorry
I'd Never Ever Felt
Haven't Found Someone To Melt
Melt On And Cover Under His Shade
To Be Saved Before I Fade
And A Nap On My Way
To Carry More Travellers With Me
And A Guy Just Gave A Glance
I Don't Know Maybe I Fantasized Romance
Wait Is That My Chance
C'mon That Ain't My Thought's Dance
Guy Made Me Stupendous
Something That God Recommend Us
Kinda Messy With Hair
But His Smile Is What I Care
And He Wasn't That Fair
But Still I Was Stupefied To Stare
And Suddenly He Just Come Here

Sitting So Near
Just The Way I Could See All Time
Till I Keep On Reading Ravindra's Line
(Ravindra Singh)
And The Ice Wasn't Broke But Melt
Something Different I Never Felt
With That Streak On His Face
The Same On Mine Like It's Traced
And That Rendezvous
Wasn't Like I Thought ToChoose
His Sight Came Upon My Book
Like It's His Soul I Took
And There We Came Talk About Love
But It's Too Low And I Was Above
I Never Fell Nor Do I Spell
I Don't Know What's Deep In Well
The Time Wasn't Slow
But I Liked It's Flow

Then The Sun Hid His Glow
And Moon Was About To Show
Such A Nice Day But Needed A Sleep
Closing My Eyes Counting 1,2,3 sheep
And I Forgot To Ask His Name
But I Thought I'll Get Later Explained
And So I Woke With A Hope
But I Wasn't Left With A Scope

He's Gone
Leaving Me Alone
But Wait He Left Somethin'
"Best Of My Times
Watching You Reading Those Lines
And Giving Me Your Glance
Talking Me; My Life's Enhanced
Love To Meet If We Had A Chance
You And Me, Unknown Friends"
And I Felt Everythin'
Deep Within
But I Can't Take Upon My Destiny
Losing His Company
And Again In The Unknown Crowd
Earphones High On Music Too Loud
Leaving Home Alone
Hiding The Tears And Clone
But Anyway He's Gone

POEMS

ANURAG NAYAK

Eager to find the words unsaid and express them. Inspired by blank pages and mind full of thoughts. An introvert turned poet.

<u>Eventually You</u>

You bluffed, went wild,
And I begged your pardon,
to make mood mild.
There you! You smiled...
Curls along your face,
I wish an excuse I had,
to touch that linen lace.
You drive me mad.
Call me worried or wise,
Won't let tears in your eyes.
It's that priceless you are,
not a cosy compromise...
Will with strength of steel
With words which could heal.
Patient as a placid lake,
A nice mom you'll make.
You walked in the crowd,
no, you lingered like a cloud.
I? Stood speechless by the lane,
Like a desert waits for rain...
Sleepless? Maybe I dreamed.
No doubts that brimmed.
Then the feelings grew,
Eventually, I fell for you.

<u>AYESHA ASIF</u>

Ayesha Asif, her full name is Bhojani Ayesha Asif. She isHailing from Maharashtra. Writing has been her way of expression. And she is addicted to novels and loves to write novels as well.

<u>Daddy</u>

For the first time wrote a poem,
As usual mommy taunted,
Brother teased,
Sisters laughed,
But there he was
Smiling as always.
Gave reward
And like always,
Dad appreciated his imperfect
little messy monster.

AYUSHI SHAKYA

I Ayushi Shakya belong to the Sangam City -Prayagraj pursuing my career in B.sc food technology, as writing was not a cup of tea for me but for a last few months I have started and now day by day my interest in this field is growing up and the encouragement of my friends over me specially Piyush Masih that helped me a lot to nurture in this field. .You can say that I'm an accidental writer.

<u>Without Reason</u>

If someone met in your life without reason
If someone messaging you without reason
Finding a way to talk to you without reason
Waiting for you without reason
Even if you talk rude
Still someone is talking to you without reason

What do you think what's that?
Attraction, friendship or love....
For me it's not an attraction, friendship or love
For me its maybe one sided love
Because first someone attracts you
Then you become friends then best friends
Then lovers (I think).
What do you think it's due to reason or without reason?

BANALI ROY

Myself, Banali Roy belonging from Chhattisgarh, (a girl from Chirmiri hills). Currently pursuing B.Sc. Food Technology from the Sangam city 'Prayagraj'.
Writing for me has always been a part of hobby since class 7th.

<u>That Chirmiri Girl</u>

She was storm in making
Collecting the bits from her past.
Moving slowly and ragging like a flash
Ready to overthrow the misconceptions.
To breakdown the stereotypes meant to guide her.
She roared with the lighting.
And became fearless like wild wind .
Oh!! But she can give life to a barren land .
And she sang with birds on the forgotten land .
A conflation of beauty and beast .
A reality that can entice .
A dream that can be the myths.
Yes!! She is a storm ready to take over the world

<u>FABBEHA KHURSHEED</u>

No matter what the situation is this girl has a key to unlock all those evils thoughts and bad moments and can transform it into reality.

<u>Oh Dear Rain!</u>

Oh dear rain!
Her ashen eyes are waiting for you endowing her love to embrace on each dew.
Clouds came floating into her life just perishing her loneliness in which she dives.

My dear rain!
You simply bring fame.
Fame for those farmers, fame for those crushed souls who cried all alone.
The mollusk are waiting for one drop to form precious pearls in the darkest curl.

Oh dear rain!
Your magical drop made the swallows circling with shimmering sound making the crops dancing on Ground.
The joy of frog in that midnight just flourishing the plum in tranclous white.

IPSITA DAS

Belonging to the state of Odisha, Ipsita Das is a Post Graduate student from Ravenshaw University. Writing is neither her passion nor hobby but just an emotional stuffs which her heart always willing to speak out.
An Amateur writer.

<u>Can I be....?</u>

Well,
I don't have a simple knowledge which can catch an attention in studies easily,
I don't have a fair complexion which can attract every people,
I don't have a perfect eyes which can catch everything very easily,
I don't have a soothing voice and proper speaking which can touch everyone's ears properly,
I don't have a tight nerves which can't be audible to me,
I don't have a perfect figure to fit in every dress,
Am I a beautiful girl?
Can I be my parent's princess?
Can I be a member of my family?
Can I be my teacher's student?
Can I be my friend's friend?
Can I be my siblings' cousin or sister?
Can I be my relatives' Twinkle (nick name)?
At last can I be accepted to the society?

KEERTHANA DHAKSHINA MOORTY

I consider myself a unicorn and spread happiness, love and positivity.

The perfect date would be stargazing,
Lying on grass wrapped with your warmth,
Hearing your stupid Stories,
Laughing at your cute lies,
Admiring your eyebrows,
Measuring my hands with your hands,
Trying your slippers on me,
Using my makeup on you,
Feeding you chillies by closing your eyes,
Seeing the way you hide your blush,
Telling you about my imaginations,
Sharing my childhood tantrums,
Playing with the Kids around,
Having silly fights,
Feeling my soul through your eyes,
Teasing you and laughing at you,
Irritating you for fun,
Feeling your love every second,
Feeling the beauty of your heart,
Feeling our souls
Connecting together.

LOKESH KALE

Hailing from Khandala, Maharashtra, and Born in business family, I have done CS, LLB, B.com, Loves to inspire to aspire more, I Write down things which I feel and as per the trend without forgetting to make people aware of their life and humanity.

Thoughts that shaped you

Oh darling why would you need to fear when I am here.

The world is beautiful when you look from the eye of a children and it is
filled with hurdle when you are surrounded by the losers near
But darling you don't need to worry because I am going to be your saviour.

Worst battle happens between the mind and the heart but for me its
between your crying eyes and your smiling face.

The easier seems to be getting harder when you disappear and the
impossible gets possible when you kiss me without any fear.

There is so much of love and peace along with hate and violence in this little
world but I find the storm and solace within your eyes my little bear.

Oh dear there is love for everyone in this world but for me it is till eternity
when you are here.
Oh dear you are a girl with some class.
A lady with Awesomness.
A lady with some Bitchnes.
A fighter with some scars.
A silent lover with so many voids.
A fierce woman with so many things in her heart.
A combination of hell and heaven.
A girl for treasure and to be a part.
A girl with so much to hide and still opens her heart.
A girl who is her daddy princess but still trust me with all her heart.
A girl who is very much loving but doesn't let apart.
A girl with so much honour and always bring the class.

So come on dear let's break this fear and I will make you my forever little
bear.

<u>MIMANSA MOHANTY</u>

Mimansa is a student currently pursuing her graduation! She is an avid reader and is a talented poetess! She occasionally loves to doodle! But generally you might find her day-dreaming or contemplating about life's mysteries!

<u>The Descended Wish</u>

The frosty skyline had given in to the freckled sunlight,
The beauty of slumber,
Gave way to lovely chirps into the sky tainted amber!
Finally, the birds took to the sky,
And the swallows danced in the high!

Ultimately, the cold feet winter had given way to the brightest summers!

It dates back to then,
13th April, 2000!
I had seen her for the very first time.
The lady with the exuberance of youth,
And her cherry eyes, the perfect balm to soothe!
She was there in the waiting, as she smiled at me,
The world didn't stand still,
But my heart did skip a beat!

This lady with Black tresses was like a fallen angel,
A twilight queen,
And a dangerously beautiful mystery I had ever seen!
Minutes later;
With that sparkle on her face,
She walked up to me,
Finally she was the lady who ADOPTED me!

A warm touch and a silent breath,
Unknown, but homely instead!
It was comforting,
I can't explain..
Ultimately, she calmed the blizzard in my head!
And from there on;
My shelter,
My mentor,
My guardian, My forever home!
She was my MOM!
She was the one for surprises,
Each day a multitude of things,
How they made me smile from toe to lips,
"Which hand was my cookie in?"

Which way would we walk to school?
Leaping over or splashing in the muddy pool!

Ever-ready she was,
Trying to find melody to my missing notes,
Forever trying to create memories,
To solace my soul!

If this isn't love,
Then what is it?
From a lost wanderer, I got my perfect fit!
From chaos to serenity,
The Girl with no name finally got her identity!

It's not the dust we come from,
Neither the dust we go to,
But the hands in our lifetime,
Ultimately, we hold on to!

MOHIT NIGAM

I'm a Biotechnologist and a self-taught artist trying to make a difference.

<u>Winter flower</u>

There was a time, in past
reality felt distant and harsh
got struck by your hair
saw seasons in your smile
your breath was warm
and your touch was fire
imagination was over
met the epitome of desire.
You're like a winter flower
no star shinier than your skin
no moment more perfect
when you look at me and smile
what can be sweeter
than honey, but your lips
read your heartbeat
and felt my fears die.

Days and night spent well
waiting for your touch
you came too close
turned my heart to gold
your love understands
what my soul signifies
and, I see my whole life
reflected through your eyes.

<u>MOKSH AGARWAL</u>

Moksh is a passionate writer and a NITIAN pursuing MCA, he as a co-writer holds a Vajra world record of world biggest Anthology which is MAPPLES published and launched in 2019, his write ups are appreciated by every reader, he mostly writes under romantic or inspirational genre, he is not a frequent writer but he is a great guide for many beginner writers.

<u>Still Mine</u>

walking down the old country lane,
Got a feeling so insane!
With this wind passing by,
Asking me if you are still mine?
The burning sun above my head
Squeezing all, making me dead!
Don't know if you are still mine
But I'll be yours for a lifetime
On my bed, with my playlist tuned
I'm on a flashback, totally screwed
I remember the dress you wore that night,
I was in front of you, on my ride!
You knew all but said none,
And my hearts scratched but I was numb.
When you leave your hair free and wild,
You look as heavenly as a baby child,
Your eyes have glitters they knew nothing about,
And cheeks were like they teased me with proud.
But with all these memories in my veins,
I just sleep with a preaching of your name.
Walking down the old country lane,
Got a feeling so insane!
With this wind passing by,
Asking me if you are still mine?

MOUMITA DAS KAR

This is Moumita,who has completed her Post- Graduation in M.A. English from Guwahati University.
Being a happy mother who loves reading and scribbling things what goes inside.

<u>Everlasting Joy of Love</u>

It's a beautiful feeling which
Inculcated in me since very long,
Of which you hardly have any thought!
Life will be really very beautiful,-
With you around me forever
When we grow really old together,
Yet our hands on hand, with smiles on lips,
We take a pleasant walk with walking sticks.
Have a thought, life will be more beautiful!
This life is as fleeting as transient-
For how long will I wait?
For how long will I not love you?
This life is for while only!
Come let's fall in love once again,
Kiss me dear once again!
I am not in my consciousness;
Not easy to resist the temptation,
So obvious in your smiles validation,
That all imagination vanishes in sublimation.
Come let's pause the night tonight,
That it doesn't breaks the dawn!
With the dawn comes a new day,
Bringing sunshine diminishing the night.
Neither Pepsi, Miranda nor coke,
Could provide me any hope!
I do really love you
Don't ever take it as a joke!
I longed long for you to exist,
I longed long for you to love,
Drench my soul so much in love,
Like I don't need to breathe again!
In the early morning gentle breeze,
Let's walk by the pathless woods,
And merge together in the magical love spree,
Amongst the rapture of trembling trees.
Although I didn't met you
In the Dawn of my life!
I am happy, as I met you;
In the sunset of my life!
Now I can sleep with a hope that,-
We will meet again forever,
In the Queen of Nights!
In the Ocean of Uncountable Wishes!

PRAKHAR PANDEY

Prakhar Pandey a writer from Gorakhpur who writes with all his heart. He gets inspired by his loved ones.
Proudly serving his nation. As a soldier he is so ambitious for his career. He loves to explore new places.
He even contributed his write-ups in few anthologies like hand-picked Poetry and stories , Elaychi etc.
And also having Vajra World Record for one of his write-up in Maples.To know about this writer you can go through his profile on instagram:
@prakhar007_bond

<u>You! Yes You!</u>

You! Yes You! You are the only star of my galaxy,
where no one is there to brighten my planet.
You are my that one cup of tea,
which always help me out to reduce my stress.
You are the flow of air that blows my hair,
the news of the day which makes me aware.
You are the stream of water
which not only touches my body but kisses my soul.
You are the one who makes me proud
and I can better find you even in the crowd.
You are the innocence of a child,
the every reason behind my smile.
You are only flower of my garden
whose essence is enough to make my day,
whose presence is enough to make my day.
You are the courage of a brave ,
The beauty of a bride,
The strength of a poor,
You will not only initiate, not only motivate,
girl you will lead, you will fight with bravery and fate.
As you told me that " I'm every present of your future"
so I wanna tell you that you are my inspiration,
you are my devotion,
As you know I'm a soldier,
baby I love you like I love my nation.

<u>PREETI BEHERA</u>

PREETI BEHERA daughter of Mr. Prabhakar and Mrs.Nandini Behera was born and brought up in Odisha.
She is 19 years old and currently pursuing English literature hons. from Khallikote University , Berhampur.
She is a passionate writer who wishes to make her passions challenge her calibre and strives to make
her parents proud. Writing is her deep heart passion as well as source of peace since from past 2 years.
She loves to relate her writings with reality.

<u>RAIN AND US</u>

The greyish clouds
up above my head
'and the greenish frondescence
in front of my eyes
are busy in flirtations,
sending lovable talks
through the colourful
dense feathers of Pavo.
She makes them happy
by dancing like a elfin
and the lightning above
miles and miles ago
acts as a melody.
Meanwhile, there came a sound
from the backside.
Darling!!!! Can you be with me
some more time??

RAKESH SINGH

Thoughts that shaped you

VeniVidiAmavi.

Hath time passed,
Did we saw?
What we felt?
What we lost?
High were the feelings with you,
Close were they when we look.
Those smiles of yours make me
Fall for you deeper than all...
Everyday i just look for you,
If every line wrote to you,
Would take your breath away.
I'll write it all.
Even more in love we'll fall.
I'll have it all.

Our love's enough,
Transcending us through space and time,
It's holding up,
It keeps you and me intertwined.

What's a pipe dream if you ain't trying to do it?
What's heartbreak if you ain't crying all through it?
What's a sunset if you ain't riding into it?
Let's drive into it.

SAKSHI AGRAWAL

She is "an incurable romantic". A nature lover and one who loves to think, dream and write. Sheadores beauty and that is the one most important driving force for life to her. Her work is an outcome of felt emotions written carefully over days of review. Hope it moves you and drives you to live.

<u>A Moment of Dissociation</u>

Lost in the darkness
Amongst the noises of silence
Things I can't understand
I want to cry
I want to shout
Perhaps break down
And seek you or someone
I want to run out of the darkness
that is draping me now.
It says it's a friend.
A silent subtle promise
that it's the most special friend I'll ever have;
But the promises are creepy
I can smell the evil
The betrayal in it
I want to run hard
Straight out of the strong hold of the darkness,
The hold that holds tight
But which promises of friendship in whispers
Only I can hear.
I can smell an enemy in its breath
As it breathes near my ear.
I can hear creepiness
in the rhythm of the air of its breath
as it slithers through my ears
and straight and full,
into the insides of my whole body
my whole lost, vulnerable being.
And I want to pursue light
I want to break out of the claws of this draping, unnerving darkness
And I know the hold is just a metaphor,
And that it never really touches me,
It never ties me through a rope,
Or prevents me, literally, from moving
But still, I just can't move.
I am free, technically;
But I just cannot grasp the strength enough to make a move or say a word
I know I want to
I know I can, technically
I try from deep inside

But it's like the depth is too deep for the push to reach my organs and my
brain.
The forces dies somewhere in the middle
It's weak,
And impotent.
Fruitless!
It's like all my muscles are out of strength,
The basic capacity of motor movement.
I know, the thing I'm staying on to is an enemy in the face of a friend,
And I know somewhere in my head,
that light exists and it is the only true friend
And I know I should run and seek light,

But it's as if the signals cannot reach my brain.
It's like I know it all,
The right and the wrong,
but at the same time I don't.
I try to run,
but I cannot walk.
Like the voice of this Enlightened Being
is somewhere so deep,
where my head cannot hear;
I feel I cannot breathe,
like all the air that I can breathe
has been stolen;
Perhaps the darkness inhales all my air
And exhales the poison for me to breathe
that is slowly killing me without even letting me know of its
conspiracy....

SAAKSHI TAILOR

I am Saakshi Tailor. Currently studying in class 12th from science stream. I started writing in classrooms and random things inspire me to write.
Writing poems have become a hobby for me. Writing things isn't a big thing all you need is some imagination and thoughts with a calm and peaceful place.
Scribbling and writing are the things which inspire me the most. Writing would have never been possible without the support of my family and friends who encouraged me a lot at every instance.

<u>Essence Of Life</u>

The window of memories
The source of memorials
The doors of your cupboard
And the wind chimes on the window
The pure flavour of life
With the heartfelt essence of love
The essence of purity
The essence of you spread over the view
The view from window of memories
The chimes on the window
Tell the story
The stories of your life
Adding fragrance to the essence
Making it being the
Perfect essence of life.

<u>SANA ERAM</u>

I am Sana Eram, a student of computer science having a hidden passion for writing. I tremendously enjoy writing poetries in both English and Urdu. Often being asked about what inspires me to write. I usually retaliate about my hidden feeling which is quite ironical for me being an extrovert. And it's actually a clash in my personality being outspoken and a dreamer too which helps me in understanding different perspectives fairly well. On an outlook, it has really helped me to grow as a person.

<u>Words So True</u>

Words so true
Gave a feeling blue
But emotions turned dark as hue
Felt like a clue
To move onto something new
To attain a better view
Even with words so true
Emotions on a brew
As it grew
It turned into a stew
Which tasted so greu
Giving it a darker view
Words with a meaning new
Provided an altered view
What appeared to be true
Was a taboo
To the feelings overdue
Out on a rescue.

SANIYA ANSARI

Hey, it's Saniya Ansari of just nineteen years. An Impulsive writer. Compulsive procrastinator.
Choses Books over Netflix.Cats overpeople.
Deemed crazy for believing in people, the little good in everything, love and being a hopelessdreamer. Wants to travel the world but also wants to sleep for an entire week.

I navigate the map of you
we walk places to places
hands entwined, minds running wild
in the purple haze of night,
our laughter fills the air,
Echoing to the canyons and
up to the sky.
We keep walking,
with destination unbeknownst
as the land awaits our feet.
And love,
love grows in untrodden pathways,
on stones and hearts and souls.
Caught between the time
we wander,
stealing glances I notice
how your eyes shimmer
how your voice quickens
and just for a while,
you let the mask slip off
you wore for others.
With wishes held between the sighs we sit,
we sit by the shore
the waves keep kissing our feet
but you don't even notice
because you look at the moon.
And I melt,
I melt into you
like a snowflake in the rain.
You make bad jokes
dance with quirky moves
In that moment
I couldn't love you more.

And it's funny how the void
I had spent years filling
with people and love and lies
and everything else transitory
Suddenly evaporated.

SARTHAK MISHRA

A writer with a smile!
I am a student who writes something you all could feel.
Likes to play basketball and write.
Happy to be alone.

<u>All I Want Is You!</u>

The way you came,
the way you stayed,
All the things became colourful
which was once fade,
I know my jokes are little lame,
But love for you will stay the same,
On my lips, there is always your name,
And I'm in love with this life's game,
Everything seems to be small infront of your fame,
I wish the essence of you will always remain,
Your presence is as sweet as sugarcane,
I always want you to be in my lane,
Our love is like huge drops of rain,
When you are not with me I become insane!

SATISH KUMAR

Hailing from the city famous for having the world's first residential
institution, Nalanda district of Bihar.
Pursing the career in B.tech Dairy Technology from Prayagraj. The
journey of writing started in an
accidental way having the hidden talent of this.

<u>Mesmerizing Eyes</u>

I looked and my eyes were stuck on you
I tried to move the black in them,
But they were stuck like glue
Looking at you for real, I noticed your eyes
That's exactly where your entire beauty lies
So genuine, so honest, so beautiful, so deep
With a glint of light, some naughtiness did creep
Finding my dream coming true
I pleaded my shivering lips
to bring out the words i had kept for you
There were so many things to say
I can't remember any of them at all
But, i don't lose with that i do things my own way...

SATISH SATYABRAT TRIPATHY

I'm Satish. I'm a MBBS student. I write sometimes.

<u>Someone Else</u>

There's no point of living for me,
And nothing to explore;
Yeah I'm afraid to die,
But don't want this life anymore.
I'm sitting here alone and seeing the sky through an open door,
Crying and smiling at the same time,
don't know what for?
Thinking about the girl I adore,
All I wish, I used to know her from before.
Every time we talk,
I feel like I'm so alive,
And every time you give me a reason to live;
But it become hard to survive,
When with someone else you arrive!

<u>MOHANTA</u>

My loneliness makes me to pen down all my thoughts. I love travelling and enjoying little things in life...

<u>Is There Anything...</u>

Is there anything
in this world without you
Is there anything
Beautiful than you
Is there anything
Important than you
Is there anything
Crazy than you
Is there anything
Emotional than you
Is there any
Achievement without you
Is there any
Lovely moments without you
Is there anything
which makes me alone
And that's nothing than My Love

SHAYAN AREEB

As I'm extremely introvert my social interaction is almost none, so most of my time goes into reading the subjects of my interest. Though I'm a post-graduate in science my passion is in reading Urdu Poetry, which in developed in my alma matter AMU and my favourite poets are Sir Iqbal & Mirza Ghalib. Taking inspiration from reading and applying it on my surroundings I use that in my writings in English, Urdu & Hindi.

<u>The Unsaid Love</u>

My heart conceals the love for you in vain,
The moment you go it makes me feel insane,
It makes me cry loud in torment and pain.
It pushes me far away from all the bliss and joy,
Your memories are like an axe to me to cut & destroy,
They make me shatter & burn like the horse of Troy.
If I will tell you my agony, you cannot bear,
I may keep on saying only if you can hear,
You may stop loving me is my only fear...

<u>SHINY JAISWAL</u>

Shiny Jaiswal, born on 4 August, 2000, is an Indian poet as well as writer.
She completed her schooling from Sunbeam School Mughalsarai in 2017.
She's pursuing B.tech in biotechnology from MGIMT,
Lucknow. She's working on her second novel with a bit darker theme. Her
pen name is Lyra Hazel.
Her first published work is co authorship in 1000 Women by Krishna Prasad.
She's featured writer at

<u>Wordsmith's mind.</u>

I write you letters,
Not of love but regret,
In an attempt of letting you go,
From my life,
Once and forever,
But I fail,
Every time I try,
To throw out,
The memories that kept me alive,
Yet I pick up the pen,
And begin another letter,
With no idea of the end,
I break down in middle,
And reach a point of no return,
I scribble away the pain,
Turning numb with each word,
Every comma and full stop,
Puts my life on hold,
And I wonder,
Do they help me to forget?
The letters I write to forget you.

SHIVANI BARANWAL

I am a writer and I just like to express my emotions through my writings.
They are not just "My write-ups"
It's a way to express my inner feelings, It is something which completes
me and moreover, If u feel
Something while reading them then my friend, it is meant for you.

<u>So Much In Love</u>

It makes me feel so special
When I see my true clearer self in your eyes,
With you holding me by your side
Grabbing me by my waist
We were totally lost in our thoughts
Just smiling and holding hands
Making promises that we will never be apart
I was so deeply lost in your mesmerising eyes
That I could even feel the numbness of my feet
But then suddenly, shocking my eyes
I realised, I was again dreaming about you
closing my eyes...

SHRADDHA UPADHYAY

Shraddha Upadhyay is a fellow at the St. Andrews College, Gorakhpur. Ambitious for her career as an
Army Officer and obviously a writer who writes about her feeling openly. She gets inspired by her loved
Ones. Shraddha loves to sing and play Guitar. She even contributed her write-ups in few anthologies like
Maples, Elaychi etc. And at the end I wanna tell you that she loves eating "Chhole Bhature".
To know about this writer you can go through her instagram profile as: @twilight_moon_maker

<u>I-M-PERFECT</u>

I know I made mistakes a lot of times,
But I love you the way Pearl shines and looks bright.
My sadness converted in anger sometimes,
And that's why I hurt you a lot of times.
Maybe, I'm not the perfect one for you,
But Baby, I love you like no one can do.
Maybe, I'm not that Princess for you,
But Baby, I will be your Queen as you always wanted so.
I am sorry for my mistakes that I had made,
I am Sorry for that eyes by which tears rolling on your face.
I make a wish on every 11:11 that,
I will be beside you or I will die for you.
Deep down from my heart I am saying that,
You are my Fate and my soul mate.
You are my Rabbit and I am your Cat,
I want to be with you till last my breath.

SHRUTI RAJ

Myself Shruti Raj. A small town girl, I would like my career to revolve around writing, which i fondly call "the
art of words" i believe in the power of words to induce change personally and globally...

<u>Mine</u>

I was the darkness
You were my light
I was lifeless
You were my life
I was the lone traveller
You were my guide
I was the fallen star
You were the clear night sky
Miles apart, million differences
As all seems to be in vain
And I was again in pain
But my love
This was not the end
As I was always yours
And you were always mine till the end...

SHWETA SINGHWAL

A Vajra World Record holder for Anthology, 3 published books and another one is in pipeline. A lady who is managing professional and house life together, working as a Sr. Merchandiser in an reputed garment Export house since 2006.

<u>Far Away</u>

Far away from here
A little hope is there,
After all pains and defeats
My Mom's love is here....

Far away from here,
A big support is there,
After all cheats and desperation
My Dad trustworthy hand is there

SUKRUTHA

An expressive extremist and an updating retrograde understanding the value of being unconditional and
understanding. Obsessed with obsessions and zeal with zest to live.

<u>Love</u>

You are no eternal but you are everything.
You are no forever but you are the first.
Anytime I am asked about love
I am more puzzled and more confused?
You know why:
Because you have been with me at my best,
Because you have been with me at my worst;
Because you have been with me at my rest,
Because you have been with me as my zest.
What you are to me love:
You were a biggest crime
I was forever a prisoner committing the crime.
You were a blessing and I was your curse.
You were all that it takes to live
But I couldn't deal without you
Because you were the life to my love
And not love of my life.
You are the breath to the beat.
You are the love I have forever never wanted to lose.

SWATI SNIGDHA BISWAL

A girl of visions. I believe in the world you be the world you create thus am in a pursuit of a better Tomorrow each day.

<u>Grave Goals</u>

Muffle drums were beating,
Family was bleeding.
The blood rolled down as tear,
The thought of losing was furiously in fear.
Mourning was all around
Only you were not on the ground.
Resting over the loved ones shoulder
Nothing was carried by you! Not even your odour.
You were the part and parcel of dust,
You would return to that dust is a must.
The ascribed attribution,
Was of no contribution
Only remembrance over the emblazon,
Was the love and affection in the live zone?
Why this" I" then??
Why not "we"
Why this materialistic gain??
When happiness is in someone's glee..
Humongous dreams in the eyes
Not letting a sound sleep,
Droplets of fantasies still breathe a soulful heap.
More acquaintances, leading minimal fervency.
Most eliteness fades with fading smile's frequency.

Earned something except money?
If yes then you owe a life honey.
Engraved merchandises decry by the ravages of time.
Inseminate mirthfulness in beings and hear the melancholy of life's chime.
The death you choose is the death you get.
Let's then desire for an earnest death goal of set.

<u>TIA KHAN</u>

I am Tia Khan, lives in Uttar Pradesh, currently doing B.Sc. (hons) from
Open University, Scotland.
Writing is my passion, my hobby, and my best friend. My favourite quote is
'Everything happens for a reason',
And yes I believe it.

<u>Love?</u>

Looking at the sky,
Because, I loved to find.
I never expected,
Anything in return.

Doesn't matter, you're with me or not,
But yes, forever in my heart.
Love, fun, care,
Is all I needed.
Only I know,
How much I miss you.
All I can do is,
To wait for you.
Daughter's first best friend,
Is always her father,
In my life,
I missed spending time with em'.
I get sad,
When I see others,
Enjoying with their father,
And I, just waiting.
Many times, I just starred,
Those moments, when we are together,
No matter, it's my birthday, or any day,
My strength, my hope, is just my father.
Love? Maybe, it's all about trust and care,
But, between a daughter-father,
Its precious one, rarest and specialist.
Love? I never knew the meaning of it, but now I knew.

Short Stories

<u>AKASH DEEP SHUKLA</u>

Coming from the city of nawabs, refining own self in the Sangam city. This is Akash Deep Shukla from Lucknow currently perusing bachelor's degree in Food Technology from SHUATS College Allahabad. Travelling and writing are one of the favourite hobbies and can be followed him on instagram as; shuklaakash8808

<u>LOVE BY COINCIDENCE</u>

 The love has defined by many peoples according to their thoughts and perceptions. If you have ever been fallen in love, you know it's not an easy task to put those feelings into words. Love is something sent from heaven to burythe hell out of you. To be brave is to love someone unconditionally, without expecting anything in return. Here, I am sharing my love story that starts with so many coincidences and still in continuation.

It was the time when the college has started in July 2016. As the first semester have been partially completed but I was not introduced with my classmates except few friends. In the very first semester of college I don't like to be regular to the classes. So my mostly practical's, assignments were pending at the end of semester. I remember the date was November 17, 2016 our respective workshop teacher said who has not completed their practical's since starting have to complete all practical's on the same day.I was happy that I got a opportunity to finish all my
Practical's on a same day. Firstly I was doing my workshop with one of my friend Tikesh but later on I was replaced with a girl. As being of shy nature, I didn't even look at her face. I completed all my work and submitted. On that day I got to know that her name is "Teena". It was just a coincidence as no one boy was in partnership with a girl for the practical work. Only I was the exception on that day. In the end of the day I was only with her name. After few days, there was a viva of electrical engineering in the department of engineering. I was seated and preparing for a viva as my id was nearby for a call. A girl who was seatingbeside me asked me help in covering her practical file as she was writing observation table in the practical copy in other one. Making her face like a cute baby she asked me for help and I was like surewhy not, I will. How can boy refuse to help a girl asking like a baby? Coincidently, while covering her file my roll call was shouted by the teacher and I left the work and went for viva. What a bad luck! I didn't even ask her name.
Finally it was the end of first semester and was with two things: first with a name of a girl and other with a face without name. Results came and second semester started. It was the very first day of the semester and no one of our batch was in the department for class. Later I was informed that mass bunk is going on. On that day, I was in the department with my friend Rohit. We both were unaware of mass bunk. It was around
11:00 am and we both were hungry. He said to me for lunch and we both left to have some food. In our university at gate no. 2 there is a food stall of various fast foods like samosa, jalebi, vada pav etc. His samosa is the biggest in our nearby university campus. While going to gate no. 2, I saw the same girl whom I met in the electrical engineering viva. I said to Rohit to ask her if she would like to come with us for some breakfast, she can join us. Luckily

she agreed to come. We had a good conversation with her. On that day I came to know that the girl who was my partner in the workshop lab and whom I saw in electrical viva was the same. It was a coincidence that in a first meeting I was with a name and second one with a face. And the both are same. One day she came to college, she was wearing a purple colour Indian traditional suit. She was really looking gorgeous. The beauty can't be defined by words. In the evening I texted her that today you were lookingbeautiful, ravishing in that purple suit. I don't know why after seeing my messages she removed her profile picture from whatsapp and no more messages were going. Later I realised that I was blocked. Afterwards we became friends and within a few months our friend circle grew up to a group of seven:Teena, Charu, Divya, Ritu, Shivani, Rohit and me. Reason behind our group formation was that we all didn't like to go anywhere in lunch. We all just keep seated in department and having fun. Once our teacher provided us with two topics, one for girls' team and other for boys. We had to give presentation

on that topic with model explanation. We all were prepared and gave our presentation. When she was giving presentation she was speaking English fluently. I was much more impressed than my teacher. When It was my turn I forgot everything in front of students whatever I prepared in English. But I gave my whole presentation in Hindi. I well-illustrated my model in front of everyone. When the result came, we both were selected as a best presenter . We all became best friends. Slowly, I was getting more impressed with her. These small events were making me feel attracted towards her. I don't even know when I fell in love with her but I was sure that mine was true. I was afraid of losing her. If I reveal my feelings then my friendship will be limited to some extent. I can't face her if she rejects my proposal. With a lot of feelings and confusions, I decided not to reveal my feelings for her. At that time, the fresher's party was going to be organised for new batch. We all were engaged in the preparation work. Coincidently, I was given work of anchoring in the party with my dream girl as a co-anchor. On 11 august 2017, the party was going on very well. On that day I don't know from where I got so much of courage and I picked up some roses from the bundle which was came for guests and I proposed her in front of my classmates.

She didn't reply anything. This all happened so sudden that we all didn't understand what happened. After that day we both didn't talked for two days but we continued our classes seeing each other faces and not saying a single word. I was feeling that I hurt her feelings. What she would be thinking about me. But things were going just opposite. She was taking time to understand me. Finally on September 4, 2017 I got my reply.

Today it's more than two year being in a happy relationship having several up and downs together. We have travelled many places as a part of our Internship training like Tamil Nadu, Himanchal Pradesh, Delhi, Darjeeling

etc. And we will visit many places in future together as it all based on coincidence.
Various people come in your life some for a short time and some for long. But whom you are attached, the value of their love, you can understand only in their absence. Even the love is not for a particular relation. It's just a purest bond between two souls.

ANUJJ ELVIIS

I'm human, I have weakness, I make mistakes and I experience sadness; but I learn from all these things I am born to be true, not to be perfect. I believe in romance. I'm not perfect, I make mistakes, and I hurt people. But when I say sorry, I really mean it. I'm actually not funny, I'm just mean and people think I'm joking.

<u>LOVE IS LOVE</u>

Vinay was a simple boy not very athletic but attractive and he could talk and charm people. He was ever smiling and always helped people. Good soul, Good heart and a hopeless romantic he could see the good in people and helped everyone, however like everyone else he too was looking for the love of his life. He was convinced that he was out there and sooner or later he will find him. He did not believe in looking for love he was an ardent follower of destiny and he wanted destiny to play its part in bringing the two together. Somewhere in his heart he was afraid to be alone. Well, but then he thought everyone is. Vinay has always been very homely and traditional in a way he was confident however still kept his innocence intact. He was naive. That day was like any other day but little did he know that it was going to turn his life around. The day, he met Raj. He got up early and rushed to the washroom to freshen upthis is was his first day at work and he did not wanted to be late on the first day of the work then he was faced with the most difficult challenge what to wear on the first day of work? You can't just wear anything and go, he thought. This was after all the first day of work. And one needs to look special onthe first day of the work. Well, he settled on that and ran outside to catch a taxi. Lucky for him his housewas on the main road that made transportation easy. He got into the cab and yelled at the driver to drive fast. He reached the office building on time and ran towards the elevator and yelled again demandingpeople in the elevator to stop it from leaving him behind. Suddenly he was pushed aside by a strangerwho yelled "sorry" and jumped in the elevator and yelled up, up and away. Well, Vinay flabbergasted,yelled back frustrated stabling himself avoiding the fall. He could not do anything as he realised he wasreally late for the first day. What will his manager think? How will his new team mates react? Multitudesof questions ran through his mind. He did not even realise that he dropped the idea of taking the elevatorand was already 3 floors on the staircase. When he reached the 4th floor he was shocked to see what hesaw! He said "what the hell" and then realized he said that out loud……..the other guy looked at him andsaid don't judge me i had a terrible night..... Vinay, did not say anything had no expressions on his facerather he hurried away from there thinking why the hell will someone change clothes in the staircase....... well, consolation was he had anamazing body. He laughed in his head and went straighttowards the conference hall. He comfortably placed himself in a chair next to someone he thoughtlooked friendly. Everyone was waiting for Mr.Oberoi to arrive he was their new Manager.   Mr.Oberoi, huh!Sounds pretty filmy he thought. And then he heard the door open and came in Mr.Oberoi with his twosecretaries who looked more like the damsels who had been rescued by him. Ten minutes in themeeting it dawned on him that he was listening to nothing but self-praise. From the corner of his eyes hesaw a shadow creeping in the conference room and slowly making its way to a chair near him. Herealized it was the same guy who he had seen in the stair case. We'll at least he has his clothes on hethought and smiled not realizing that the guy was looking at him and smirked. Meeting over andeveryone jumped on the coffee machine so did he. Hey! New guy, so you like checking people outchanging clothes? He was embarrassed it was the guy behind him. Hi, I am Jatin your crush. Wait what excuse said Vinay. Jatin laughed and said chill dude i am just taking your case think of it as new hireragging. Anyway let me show you where you are sitting come with me and don't worry I won't take myclothes off i know you want me too... very funny said Vinay but to your surprise i don't and was not evenchecking you out in the staircase and anyway who changes there. And they started chatting and soonVinay realized that maybe after all Jatin was not that bad. He had a good first day made a lot of new

friends courtesy Jatin. Seems Jatin was the office Casanova and favourite.

At the end of the day Jatin walked up to Vinay's workstation and said its Raj's birthday everyone is goingto the party and he should come. Vinay refused at first but later gave in and headed towards Raj'sapartment to attend his birthday party. The room was dark and soft music played and Vinay wassurprised as he had never seen a human sushi platter. He got over his shock when everyone laughed andwished happy birthday to Raj. Soon Vinay found himself introducing himself and wishing happy birthday

to raj covered in sushi. Well, this is new he thought. Anyway he tried not to stare but managed a glancesmiled and walked away.

Later fully clothed Raj walked in and celebration was in full swing while Vinay was in the balcony sippinghis beer alone. Hey don't feel outcast your among friends he heard from behind it was Raj. Thank you,said Vinay. Well, you look good with clothes on also and they both laughed and clicked instantly, soon

they both realized that it was 3 in the morning and everyone had already left and they were alone. Rajinsisted on him staying the night. Well what had left of it anyway as tomorrow was a weekend.Vinay woke up to astounding smell of coffee with toast and sunny side up omelette just the way he likeshis breakfast. Hey! Good morning something about you told me you are a sunny side up guy so I tookthe liberty I can change if you're not said raj. No, I am said Vinay and smiled. Soon they stared meetingoften and grew closer. Vinay did not even realize but soon they were sharing an apartment. You knowthe feeling when you just met the person and feel that you have known each other for ages were thefeeling that both shared. Anyway days turned into weeks and weeks to months and they grew closer andcloser and much in love. It was a bright Sunday morning they were with friends and Vinay noticed thatJatin's phone kept on buzzing and he seemed to avoid it and then he excused himself and took to a corner and started talking on his phone for about an hour when he returned everyone asked if everythingwas ok? Yes everything is ok and they all went on as usual. Later, Radha a colleague said so Jatin do youknow who is in town? Jolly, do you think you guys will meet? Jatin just shrugged. That evening whenJatin was in the restroom his phone buzzed again and though Vinay wanted to avoid looking he stillManaged a peak and saw a dozen missed called from someone called Jolly! Something made him upset and worried but he did not react later he confronted Jatin as to who was Jolly but did not get an answer.This puzzled Vinay even more. Seeing that Jatin was not going to tell him one night he sneaked into hisphone and read messages from Jolly they were loving demanding messages clearly Jatin was twotiming him he thought and later picked up a fight with him Jatin said he had to trust him but he did notlisten and the broke up. He was heartbroken and thought how could he do this to him he gave his all tothis relationship. Almost a month passed and neither of them could live without each other but bothwere as arrogant asthe other and refused to talk. They started avoiding parties and clubs to as to avoidbumping into each other but fate had a different design. Radha was not well and Vinay was caretaking her. And that's when she told him about Jolina who was Jatin's evil step sister straight out of rehab andnow again slipping who was pestering Jatin for money. Wait! What Jolly is a girl thought Vinay and itdawned on him that how stupid he had been to let true love go away because he was insecure and hadtrust issues he loathed himself and broke down not knowing what to do? He had literally crushed hisown love life and now had nothing. Almost a year had passed and his friends pushed him to go clubbingto which he agreed and bumped into Jatin there. No words were exchanged they only lip locked foreternity and ever since had been together.

<u>AROMA GUPTA</u>

Aroma Gupta is belonging from Prayagraj, city of sacred rivers. There is nothing special about her, she is a common Indian girl with inbuilt Indian values with high dreams and biggest desire to fulfil it. Now she is on the way to complete it as she is doing bachelors of homoeopathic medicine and surgery from VNSG university, Surat, Gujarat

<u>OUR FICTITIOUS SON</u>

As we usually call him "Annav", but grammatically correct he is "Arnav". Though his name was suggested by his papa and the very little job done by my side to ethereal him. As his papa loves child a lot so we Fiction's our own, we decided to name him "Arnav", he is extremely naughty one with fair complexion, having chubby checks with cutest smile and a humpty Dumpty type tummy with a round palm, some curly brownish hairs and pure black pupil with full of love & affection. So the story to dream up goes this way....

It was 12:55 am and I was on my study table concentrating on my physiology book, suddenly a message popped, "HI MAA".
I saw the profile picture and it was he (Arnav),
I replied, "HELLO BABY" then i took my silver bookmark and used to keep my place in the book to enable me to return to it with ease and switched off the lights and got on my bed.
He said with cuteness "MUMMA.... I WANNA SLEEP ON YOU" "HOW YOU WILL COME TO ME, ITS 12:59 am BABU", I replied,

He: "WITH THE HELP OF MY ANYWHERE DOOR MAA" "WOW", MAY I USE YOUR DOOR TOO, I replied
He: "NO MUMMA YOU ARE TOO FAT AND MY DOOR IS TINY NA, AND IF YOU INSIST ITS GONNA BE BURST SOON" with some naughtiness and chats started Definitely messages are send by his papa but it seems beyond the reality, we kept on chatting day after day.
He is only 4 years old, and I forgot to mention that he is more interestedin females as his papa is, he has 2 girlfriends from school, on one hand "Vedika" he call her "Vedu" and on another "Simran", they both are cute and most beautiful girls after his mumma. He is food Connoisseur, His love fluctuates per day depending on the type of lunch they bring for him, he got totally confused with whom he going to marry. Sometimes he asks to me "maa who is better for me".

"None, as one is prettier and another is smart but no one have both the qualities like me", I replied.

Without saying anything he started staring at me.....even right this moment he have a gun to my head (Hahahaha).Then together we laugh a lot and have a tight hug hmmmm.............he kisses me like I'm his favourite teddy bear and he punches his papa like he is his favorite boxing bag. Whenever he got to know that his papa hurts me, no matter for what or in which situation, immediately he start pulling his papa's hair and give lots of punches, right after his papa apologize for something that he was done.

Thoughts that shaped you

As cytogenetically child carry more of their mother's genes than their father but in our case Arnav shows more characters of his papa. Here only I'm jealous with my man.

Somewhere he become a piece of our body, he goes everywhere with his papa and hide himself in papa's pocket. He loves to blow horn continuously when papa is driving. He wants every little pack of things, one day he insist to have a specs like Mumma, on the same day I bought little specs for him, he used to put it on papa's driving seat to watch Papa every time.

Generally couples dream up that their child will first say mumma or papa but in our case Arnav's first word is "amma (grandma)", she is everything for him, from sunrise to sunset if anyone who cares for him is only amma. Although we are parents and he love us fullest but amma is priority for him, he used to jump on amma's tummy and feel safest on her arms.
Helove to visit on his grandpa house because grandpa hold him in his arms and took him to a long ride and make him happy with all outside fast foods, definitely his upbringing had done by his grandparents.

He is patriotic by nature he has the feeling of love, devotion and sense of attachment to a homeland and alliance. This attachment can be a combination of many different feelings relating to his own homeland, including ethnic and cultural. Whenever at any time he heard national anthem sung by anyone he just stand up straight with respect outside in open area under the sky. He dreams to join in Indian army sometimes but his Papa wants to see him to become a successful cricketer who will playing world cup 2045 "India vs. Pakistan" hosted by England and to be a man of the match, and here I want to see Arnav as a successful surgeon qualified by a reputed government college. But we never gonna forced him to make our dreams come true, he has his own dreams and potential to make it true, the thing only we want is to be a successful person in his life no matter what it be.

Whenever we planned to go for shopping, Arnav's long list would be ready for marketing, he loves to do so and he wants everything more than a dozen, and the priority is to take a meal outside on the same day, his most favourite "maharaja Mc meal" in McDonald is mandatory, he nibble slowly and took much time to finished it all.

Slowly day after day Arnav become a part of our life, our hearts beat for one another, we generally say on one hand Arnav and his Papa is not 2 different person they both are same on another Arnav and me arealso same, our small family is much more prettier than the heaven.

On every morning I wake up with then message popped in my Whatsapp Messenger "good morning maa" and every night I sleep after hugging him and say "good night baby", we usually chat using emojis. Whenever we decided that Arnav is with his Papa then Papa is the only one who is playing role of Arnav at that time and when Arnav is with me then I'm the one who become Arnav to chat with his Papa, that we both are satisfied by talking to their son every day.

The most beautiful moment of my life when his Papa introduced his obscure son to me as if my heart never met that much of peace. Only we felt that he is in front of us but we are helpless that we can't touch him because we have a kind of mirror wall in between us.

We are at our own career shapers and waiting limitless for the day come when Arnav's really become a part of our life for the lifetime.

<u>AYUSHI AHUJA</u>

My name is Ayushi Ahuja.
I am currentlyperusingpost-graduation inMA literature from GDC College.
My hobbies aredancing, writing stories poetries, listening music andcrafting.

<u>PRIORITY</u>

Shreyansh and Ahana were lovely couples and loved each other so much but Shreyansh was always busy in his work due to which there relationship was kind of lost somewhere. Next week Ahana's birthday was coming so Shreyansh decided to surprise her at midnight but due to work load he wasn't able to go there so he decided to send her cake and flowers through one of his friend. So he called his friend Rohit and asked him to do so and he agreed. It was almost midnight and few minutes were left for Ahana's birthday. Ahana was waiting for Shreyansh call. Suddenly, Doorbell rang Ahana thought it was Shreyansh who was there for her to give her surprise but when she opened the door she was shocked to see Rohit because it was almost midnight but when Rohit told her that Shreyansh asked him to deliver these to her then she relaxed for bit. Ahana stayed alone at her flat because she was also staying away from home because of her job. So It was a scary scenario for her to have someone unexpected at her flat. To confirm she immediately called Shreyansh and he explained his reasons to Ahana that why he wasn't able to come. Ahana was bit scared and the way Rohit was looking at her was also giving her negative vibes. Then before leaving Rohit asked Ahana for water. When Ahana turned to get water Rohit fasten her frombehind. He hit Ahana's head on wall and she passed out. When she came back to her senses she was lying on the floor and all of her cloths were taken away. Somehow she managed to stand up because she was suffering multiple injuries on her body and head. It was looked like Rohit tried to kill her before leaving. She called Shreyansh a multiple times but Shreyansh didn't attend her calls because of his work. He thought he will call her later after finishing his work. When even Shreyansh wasn't there for her. She broke deep inside and the incident gave her a huge shock and at that very moment she jumped from her building and committed suicide. But it was a MURDER. MURDER of her FEELINGS MURDER of her TRUST MURDER of her CONSCIENCE The lessons we get from the above story are: - Never avoid your loved ones and give them your first priority.(if Shreyansh have attended her calls maybe she Wouldn't have committed suicide) Do not trust others blindly. (If it was impossible for Shreyansh to go there that night he should have done it some other time rather than trusting someone this blindly.

KRISHANU DEB

Hi, I am an advocate by profession, an avid writer, photographer by passion. Writing always gave me the world i wanted in my mind, it gave wings to my imagination. My ideas of writing always try to explore something abstract from being regular.

<u>THE WOVEN HEART</u>

2nd Dec, a beautiful winter morning, in fact a lazy morning for everyone, the calmness inside the room suddenly got distracted by the sound of words, "GET UP GET UP, it's 9:30" "Yes mom a few minutes more was the prompt reply". No get up now and take shower, don't you know we are going to the temple this morning get up now. Uff!! These moms I tell you sometimes behave in such a way as if she is going to miss a flight for that few minutes. So after the oral application for the extension of a few more minutes got rejected she had no other options but to get off the bed, she walked like a lazy snail towards the window. Ahaa! The moment she opened the window a sweet misty fragrance of fog along with the cool breeze started flowing inside the room kissing the curtains and making them dance to their tune. Oh! I forgot let me introduce you all to myself, hi everyone I am RICK, beautiful name Na? She lovingly gave me the name and I too love it when she calls me every time by this name and introduces me to her friends, by the way the girl I am talking about is AASHI. Aashi and I both know each other for a very long time, and our relation deepened along with the passing of time. I still remember the first day i saw her, a beautiful girl with a sweet smile on her face walking towards me and befriending me among all others. Slowly and certainly our bonding grew so strong that she always spoke her heart out only in front of me. In joy she would give me a tight hug and a sweet kiss and when sad she would hug me and cry until she found some comfort. Yes today is a very special day for her and for me too, for her it is because today is her birthday and for me because exactly one year before on this day I met her. So everyone in the house were excited including myself for the party in the evening, lots of guests and friends are going to attend the celebration. As the evening wore on the guests started arriving all beautifully dressed up, the tempo was slowly taking its speed, and within a few minutes a beautiful chorus song with wishes for the birthday girl filled up the hall. I was so happy with the smile that was glowing on her happy face, may god keep that smile glowing every time, a small wish that came from my heart, i wanted to but couldn't express my wish. Even though I was aware of her love for me still something was there that was coming in between me and her. Whatever it was, one thing that I was happy about was the fact that right from the first day of our meeting I was the only one till now who remained so close and special to her and sure enough that it shall continue all throughout the life. All these thoughts distracted my heart for a moment from the surroundings until Aashi came closer to me and kissed me introducing some of her new friends to me. Meet my sweet love his name is Rick, Aashi told her friends, Uff some of her friends were touching my cheeks; I didn't like that at all. Don't do that making some distance from them Aashi told her friends, her possessiveness for me gave me a shivering joy all through my deep inside. All of a sudden a boy sitting by her side got up, "I need to tell you something" he whispered, alright friends lets go to my room Aashi told them, holding me by her side. As we were climbing the upstairs, something went throughout my mind, mm what does the boy wanted to tell her probably even Aashi herself didn't had any idea about that or perhaps may be. Once we entered her room all her friends sat on the bed and some on the chair or floor, my sit was in front of her dressing table. I could very well notice a certain expression and eye contacts in between all her friends and Aashi too. But couldn't understand what was that, "you wanted to tell something" looking towards the boy Aashi asked him. Ok everyone I have got something to say please listen, having said that the boy slowly came walking towards Aashi. He put his hand inside his pocket and took out a beautiful ring, "I LOVE YOU AASHI, I BROUGHT THIS RING AS A TOKEN OF LOVE, WILL YOU ACCEPT IT" he said holding her hand. "YES, I DO AAKASH" Aashi replied, i couldn't believe my senses what was going on, never ever I felt so bad like that moment. Everyone present there got up with joy and started hugging each other with joy except me, Aashi didn't even cared to look towards me, perhaps someone has already taken my place in her heart. As I was thinking all this, my eyes went towards the mirror that very reflection of the mirror gave all the answers of the questions that were running in my minds. A sense of realization cleared the fog from the mind, with the heart giving the answer RICK everyone loves you, even you can also fall in love with everyone but the only difference is that your heart is not pumping blood like others, nor does it's beats increases or decreases unlike others which helps them to express their feelings freely. For your HEART IS WOVEN with cottons and threads, whatever names you are given or called by others but still at the end of the day you are a TEDDY BEAR, a toy for everyone and an imaginative companion for those who loves you. Never ever I felt so much lighter in comparison to others, everything that started silently one day, got drowned inside the sea of deep silence forever. Yes this me RICK and this is my story, A Love story of mine and special moments of my life which was, is and always shall remain unexpressed for everyone, until someone somewhere someday releases that even a TEDDY BEAR can fall in love.

RAGHURAJ SINGH RAJPUT

A poetizer never quits best define me.
Myself Raghuraj Singh Rajput from Lucknow.
I am a UPSC aspirant. I love to write with my pen name 'raghu' in Hindi.

<u>A TALE: RELAXING WITH PAIN</u>

"Castle in the air castle in the air why did you say you are very rare?" This question has lost itsidentify just because it is a question. As the social media plays a very important role in our life but how much importance it has been imprinted on me specially in this case I don't know. No, don't think that I'm going to tell you about the 'Broad-band' connection between me and some social sites. The twos has been misused by and at their

Height. After my boards, I came to village from Lucknow with having folded and unfolded friendships. It was 10th of April and the day was not freaky and everything was going very conducive in its way. I had having a conversation with my friend on social site naming Whatsappthen a name stuck in my mind it wasn't just a name it was loaded on with lots of feelings for me. Whenever I listen up her name my heart beat increases till now it does the same. I took her contact from my two friends, Arnav and Shikha, they deserve an effusive thank. Arnav is a decent boy and a good friend of mine and it is the much describing character in my story. The story is nothing for 'everyone'. She was my old classmate how old she was I can't say because this fact ruined its own inception when I texted her after six months of last met up. The girl having purest form of voice, in one word 'melodious' and her smile always pulls me from the tag of shy one to the tag of talkative one. Sometimes I felt that I'm a professional joker and her little angry face makes me to make her more angry. All just carried innocence and an 'unbreakable' bond between us. But the bond had its own weakness and that

weakness doesn't allow me to write her name. Just P. On mentioned day, I texted her a message andwaited very lovingly for her reply the reply came at midnoon when I was sleeping the phone increased my heart beat volume and having her online speed up my fingers. The network was slow but the typing speed was fast I just came out from room to had good network and it worked actually." I must say she defeated in everything from texting to owning her." On that day I was so happy. By the time my love towards one is increasing and for one is decreasing.

The day was just the inception of being an owner of my 'own' melancholia. From that day we started talking about every day in fact I was not talking I was feeling but didn't make a phone call till 17th of May. On 17th, I was in bank having mom for few works. P called me.My heart beat was pumping high that anyone could felt that but anyhow I talked just talked about usual things. But on next day, my happiness vanished as I messaged her but didn't get a reply and my whole day went into vain. At night, I pen downed what I felt and I think that day kept an inception for being a writer. I thought am I doing the act of perfidy to me or she because 'Blue tick' without having reply hurt a lot. We had lots of talks and the huge crush which I had from early class was on its height but I continued to talk and didn't say about my feelings it was my 2nd mistake 1st was continuing to talk her. The days had started to come in way having nothing but sadness. On my birthday she wished me at about 5 pm I was so angry but still thanked her because her wish made my remaining day and night good as it was the first good thing that happened on that day. I thought that I would propose her on her birthday Aug 9. But I lost every connection to talk her I was unable to find any clue that how could I talk her because I got to know that she was using her maternal aunt's phone so I restricted myself to do message often. I hadfaith in her that she will contact me as her assurance of waiting me made me to stand with the confidence that yes she will. But they were just words nothing happened according to that. I'm still waiting to meet her after passing two years but not lovingly. We had next conversation after five days of my birthday. Those days were hardest for me to being with me. The days were passing and I festered and giving me the mental illness. At that time I uninstalled and reinstalled Whatsapp about 20 times in just 7 days and did it many times in 3 to 4 months. That mental illness made me to write more and more this was only good thing. On 9th Aug, I wanted to put a status on Whatsapp and wanted to call her but the main thing happened. The mentioned 'boy' Arnav...I was little bit touched by with their unknown story (unknown for me only). He put status which made me to not to do the same. I made a phone call to him at night and asked about entire tale. He told me about everything like I was telling him about my story but the main thing which he kept away from me was 'rejection'. She rejected him but kept talking to him just to avoid the fear of losing a good friend. We can't generate feelings if we can't feel. Feelings that are something which pour out from our heart automatically for someone not for everyone. From that conversation which went about 63 min with Arnav I remember one thing only that I said "Brother I'll convince her for you". What happened to me to say so I don't know but I became a villain for me that I knew. By the time that 'mini' sacrifice is loaded on with the 'ignocare'(ignorance+care). I knew that I can't say by my side but still I hoped him and from that day I kept advising him. I murdered my feelings for him actually I didn't but in eyes of Arnav I showed that I was nothing. But the crush is the thing whichremains forever. I had lots of complications those days I felt like I was alone in the desert full of storms. The loneliness was Killing me. I became so rude that I started hating everyone. Many a times I ignored her but whenever I thought to go away I felt that I came closure. Fluctuations came in our talking but whenever I talked her my emotions evoked every time. We had lots of fights and I remember when I talked her so rudely that she told me no one talked like you in my entire life. I was so angry on myself but still I did just because I wanted she start hating me. I did lots of things which made her to not to talk with me. The problem is not of having her but the problem is of losing a good friend. Arnav, she and me we are good friends but feelings can't be burned with the tag of friendship. I did a lot for Arnav to have her but she has another better half. If someone is happy with someone else then let them. I had no regrets in last but a thing which pierce me when I think that she was known by third person about my feelings and she told me that if you had told me about yourself I might think about you. We had made lots of misperceptions about each other. As I was introvert so how could I have crush on her remains a question for her. Today, we rarely talk and don't make phone calls also having each other contacts but we know we can't block each other on any social sites. This is something 'different'. Sometimes my self-respect demanded some respect but I slapped it every time. "Again I woke up with my 'own' melancholia again I thrashed by with my own destiny."

RICHA CHUGH

Richa Chugh aged 28 years thalassemia warrior, from Faridabad(NCR), Haryana. Completed her Post Graduation in finance. A Published author who loves to ink her emotions and writes poems, quotes,
microtales on different topics varying from social issues to inspirational musings and also interested in making handicraft items. A person with crazy mind yet a positive soul is apt to describe her. Contact her on
Gmail: rc.inkdiary@gmail.com
Instagram: rc_inkdiary

<u>RAIN</u>

Rain is what welcomed me the moment I stepped out, all though it's mid monsoon and it's ok to rain anytime and everytime but still I was expecting for it not to rain today, at least for these few hours..The hours of my drive with Rihan.

Anyway I made my way towards the parking tagging Rihan along, entered my car, somehow managing to not get drenched. And began my drive. The drive I religiously take every year on this particular day.

Few minutes into the drive, accompanied by the rain. I was travelling to the past. The past which made this day so unwanted to me. For I gained or I lost, i still can't contemplate.. The Roads, The lush green trees, nothing could take of my attention but the rains. Why I can't ignore rains is something I still don't have an answer to..

After 3 hrs I took a break. Out of the city. Roadside tea stall were his favorites, I never loved them but Rihan was just like him. Impatient, excited and always on the edge. I stopped my car and got down. While I ordered for a masala tea and let Rihan played around..

After a break and good amount of relaxation.. We were back on road. Time flied with music and it was lunch time. And finally we reached there the place, our destination.

Rihan immediately recognized it and was impatient enough to let me park. I opened the door and he jumped out. I parked the car, came out.

Sitting on the bench I ordered for Tea.

Sadness engulfed me. The day 5 year back flashed and I was numb.

We were a happy family. Me, my wife Madhu and our 5 year old Rihan(my son). We were coming back from a wedding and stopped on a roadside dhaba for lunch. It was drizzling and the weather was very nice

Rihan was excited, he was playful and inquisitive about everything. Papa what is this, papa what's there. I tried answering him for a while and then told him to play on the hill side. He went there and started his kid play. I could see him laugh, play and run around in rain.

Me and Madhu ordered tea and sat on the bench chit chatting, throwing glances on Rihan time to time and then relaxing. We were happy, and content seeing our child so happy. And suddenly I hear him shout

"See papa, baby Rihan"

He was running behind a puppy. And was calling him baby Rihan. I went to him and started playing with both of them.

Amidst the conversation i asked him

"Rihan, I can't keep two Rihan na. I'll take one of you home."

"Then take him dadda, he is small"

Came the innocent reply

I couldn't control but smile. After playing for some time. I brought them to the dhaba to have food. I bought milk and biscuits for baby Rihan and some tasty Paranthas for my baby Rihan. They both were happily nibbling on their food. So were we. Me and Madhu were glad that Rihan found a company and were planning to take the puppy home. Discussing all this we didn't realised when they both sneaked out to play.

All we heard after few minutes were huge shouts and cries.

We ran out and were shocked. There was an accident. And...

My baby Rihan, My little 5 year old was lying on road drenched in blood and rains. He held little puppy tightly in his hand and I lost my balance. It took me 30 seconds to realise what had happened and I rushed to him.

"Baby, what happened" i picked him up..

"Dadda this baby Rihan was running on road. You said you will take one of us home. You take him..." and that was last he spoke..

I was down on my knees, my baby in my arms lifeless with open eyes still asking me to take care of his baby, whom he was still holding tight.

The crowd later told Rihan ran in front of a car to save the puppy and got hit. I couldn't believe.. My little one left us. Just like that..

We were back home, my family preparing for Rihan's last ceremony..Madhu was in shock. She won't cry, she won't speak..

And I hear a whimper.. I see that little puppy sitting right besides Madhu's feet and nibbling. And that was it. Madhu picked him up. Hugged him and cried, cried for long 3 hours. And I couldn't stop her.

All I knew was I need to take care of my baby's baby and we had our Rihan back...

"Sir Tea!!"

I was startled, the memory lane became hazy and i saw a boy handing me the tea cup.

I looked around and saw Rihan sitting at the roadside in the rain, seeing across the road.

He remembers him, He does just like we do..

"Hey baby Rihan come back, time for biscuits"

And he came running to me...

Rihan never left us. He was there, there with me in the Rains...

<u>SPECIAL THANKS</u>

Special thanks to the two most important persons who helped me a lot through this entire project.

SUBUHI IQBAL

The only person who could get the credit of everything which I am doing either in studies or in extra-curricular. The one who made me become capable of doing things the right way. No matter how much the difficulties may come but she has always been the one who stood by my side. The mentor, the guide and the one who is much more than a family to me.

RUBAL CHOUDHARY

Being a total acquaintance to each other but still she helped me a lot throughout the project, being the guide she guided me at each and every end. Thank you so much for the efforts you showed during the entire project.